BLUEBERRY MUFFIN'S BOOK
An Adventure in Blue

by F. S. Kim

Scholastic Inc.

New York   Toronto   London   Auckland   Sydney   Mexico City   New Delhi   Hong Kong   Buenos Aires

ISBN 0-439-70468-5

Designer: Emily Muschinske
Illustrations: Lisa and Terry Workman
Photographs: F. S. Kim
Gabe Houser, Grace Houser, Megan Hines, and Jennifer Smalls
are pictured in the photos on pages 35 and 37.

12 11 10 9 8 7 6 5 4 3 2 1   5 6 7 8 9 10/0
Printed in the U.S.A.
First Scholastic printing, February 2005

TABLE OF CONTENTS

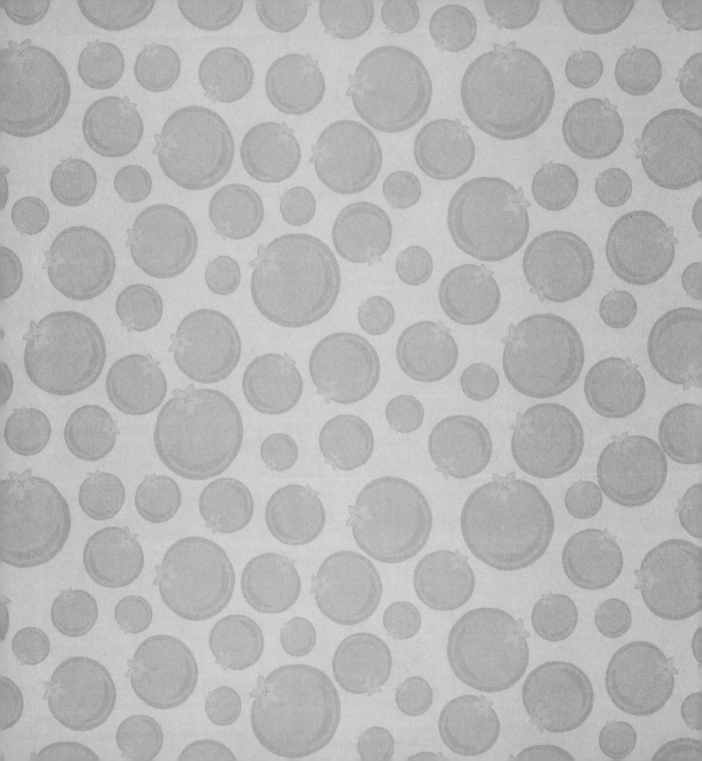

Get Ready for an
ALL-MUFFIN ADVENTURE!

Hi, it's me, Strawberry Shortcake, and my berry special friend, Blueberry Muffin.

Welcome to Blueberry Valley! I live here, in a muffin-shaped house, with my pet mouse, Cheesecake. I make the best muffins in all of Strawberryland, with fresh blueberries picked from the bushes right outside my home!

Join us on a blueberry adventure filled with berrylicious crafts, recipes, and games!

Are you ready? Grab your Blueberry Craft Kit and let's go!

Blueberry Muffin and Strawberry Shortcake's Tips for Getting Started

1. Cover your work space with newspaper to keep it clean and neat.

2. It's a berry good idea to gather everything you'll need before you start a new project or recipe.

3. Whenever you see this symbol in the book, it means you can find what you need in your craft kit.

4. You can find the other materials you'll need for the projects in your local craft or grocery store.

5. You'll need a grown-up's help on some of the projects in this book. When you see this symbol, you'll know to ask for help.

Berry Funny

Q: Why was the strawberry scared?
A: It saw a boo-berry!

Getting Ready to Make the Recipes

Many of the recipes in this book use fresh blueberries. Here are a few tips:

1. Wear an apron or a smock when you're making a recipe, since blueberry juice can stain.

2. Look for blueberries that are large and firm. They'll be berry juicy!

3. Sort through your blueberries before you start a recipe to make sure there aren't any bad ones. Wash the berries in cold water.

4. Wash your hands with soap and water before starting a recipe.

Getting Ready to Use Yarn and Pom-poms

Many of the crafts in this book use yarn and pom-poms that come in your craft kit. Here are a few tips:

1. It's easiest to cut yarn if you pull it tight first. Then use good scissors to cut it.

2. When you're finished using your yarn, wind it up neatly and put it away. This will keep it from getting knots and tangles.

3. When you're gluing two pom-poms, use your fingers to squeeze the pom-poms together, then slowly count to ten. This will help the pom-poms stick together better.

4. You'll use a lot of glue when working with yarn and pom-poms. You might need to add more glue later if the yarn or pom-pom doesn't stick.

Turn the page to make a berry juicy picture!

Basket of Blueberries

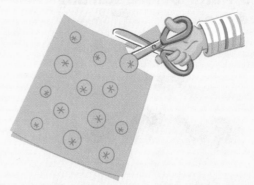

Blueberries are Blueberry Muffin's favorite fruit. These blueberries look good enough to eat!

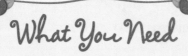

What You Need

- 2 sheets of construction paper (pink and blue)
- Pencil
- Ruler
- Blue crayon or marker
- Scissors
- White glue or craft glue
- Green yarn

2. With a blue crayon or marker, draw some round blueberry shapes on your piece of blue construction paper.

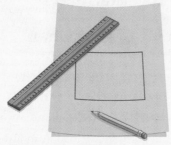

1. Lay down a pink sheet of construction paper the tall way. Sketch a 3-x-4-inch box in the center of the paper with a pencil and ruler. This will be the outline of your basket.

3. Draw dashes inside each blueberry to make a star. Cut the blueberries out.

4. **Glue your blueberries to fill the box you made on the pink construction paper. Place some blueberries above the top line of your basket, so it's all filled up with blueberries!**

5. **Cut four 4-inch pieces of green yarn. Glue one piece of yarn on the top and bottom of your blueberry basket, and glue two pieces of yarn in the middle to make four lines.**

6. **Cut four 3-inch pieces of green yarn. Glue one piece of yarn on each side of your basket, and two more pieces in the middle to make a grid as shown. Let dry.**

Here's More: You can fill up your basket with strawberries or raspberries! Use pink paper to make your berries and fill your basket with them.

Turn the page to make a card that's a berry sweet surprise!

A Berry Sweet Card

Use yarn to make strawberries and blueberries for a card that's berrylicious!

2. With your pencil, sketch five blueberries and five strawberries on the front of your card, any way you like.

What You Need

* 1 sheet of light-colored construction paper
* Pencil
* Crayons
* Yarn (pink, blue, and green)
* Scissors
* White glue or craft glue

3. Color in your strawberries and blueberries with crayons. Make a little star with little lines on your blueberries. Color seeds and leaves on your strawberries.

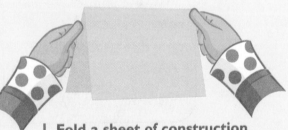

1. Fold a sheet of construction paper in half.

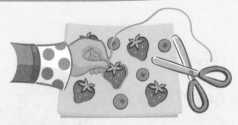

4. Take your pink yarn, and lay it over the outline of a strawberry, as shown. This will show you how much yarn you need. Cut the yarn with scissors.

7. Use green yarn to make loops to outline a strawberry's leaves. Cut the yarn, then glue it into place. Repeat for the rest of the strawberries.

5. Outline your strawberry with glue, and place your pink yarn over the glue. Repeat steps 4 and 5 with all the strawberries in your picture.

6. Take your blue yarn and measure it around a blueberry. Cut and glue the yarn to make an outline for the blueberry. Repeat for the rest of the blueberries.

Here's More: Write "Have a Berry Nice Day!" inside your card and give the card to a friend as a surprise!

What's blue, polka-dotted, and fun to wear? Turn the page to see!

Blueberry Muffin's Polka Dot Bracelet

You can make and wear this bracelet to match Blueberry Muffin's cute polka-dotted cap!

What You Need

- Toilet paper tube
- Scissors
- White glue or craft glue
- Blue yarn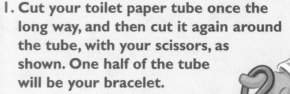
- Penny
- 1 sheet of light blue construction paper
- Pencil

1. Cut your toilet paper tube once the long way, and then cut it again around the tube, with your scissors, as shown. One half of the tube will be your bracelet.

2. Squeeze a line of glue on the front edge of the bracelet. Press the end of the blue yarn over the glue. Let dry.

3. **Wrap the yarn around the bracelet to cover it, making sure that the yarn lies flat. You can rewrap the yarn if you make a mistake.**

4. **When there's no more bracelet to cover, squeeze a line of glue on the front of the bracelet, and stick the yarn to it. Cut off any extra yarn. Let dry.**

6. **Glue the circles all over your bracelet for polka dots. Let dry. Slip your wrist into the slit in the back to wear your new bracelet!**

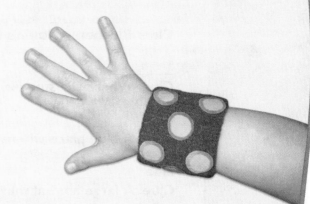

5. **Use a penny to trace small circles on a sheet of light blue construction paper with a pencil. Cut the circles out.**

Here's More: Squeeze a little glitter glue on the dots to add some sparkle to your bracelet.

Can you guess what Blueberry Muffin's favorite color is? Turn the page to see!

Blueberry Muffin's Blue Words

Blueberry Muffin likes things that are blue. Can you guess what these blue words are based on the clues? Look around these pages to see if you can spot a picture of the word you might be looking for.

1. __ __ __ __ __ __ __ __ __ __ __ __
   Clue: **Blueberry Muffin's favorite fruit.**

2. __ __ __
   Clue: **Where the sun and clouds stay.**

3. __ __ __ __ __
   Clue: **A blue place where water animals live.**

4. blue __ __ __ __ __
   Clue: **A large animal that lives in the sea.**

5. blue __ __ __ __ __
   Clue: **A kind of pants that are usually blue.**

6. blue __ __ __
   Clue: **A bird whose name sounds like a letter of the alphabet.**

Answers on page 38.

Turn the page for some fun
with pom-poms!

Blueberry Muffin's Cute Mouse, Cheesecake

Make your own little mouse that looks just like Blueberry Muffin's best pet pal!

1. Lay all the pom-poms on your work space. You should have two large pom-poms, two medium pom-poms, one small pom-pom, and a tiny pink pom-pom.

What You Need

- 2 large (1 1/2-inch) light blue pom-poms
- 2 medium (1-inch) light blue pom-poms
- 1 small (3/4-inch) light blue pom-pom
- 1 tiny light pink pom-pom
- White glue or craft glue
- Colored pencils
- White construction paper or card stock
- Scissors

2. To make Cheesecake's body, squeeze a dime-sized spot of glue on top of one large pom-pom. Place the other large pom-pom on the glue, and press the two pom-poms together. Count to ten. Let dry.

3. Glue the two medium pom-poms on the sides of the top large pom-pom for ears. Let dry.

4. Take the small pom-pom and glue it on the front of the large pom-pom for a mouth. Glue the tiny light pink pom-pom on top of the mouth for Cheesecake's nose.

5. With colored pencils, draw two small paws, two round eyes, a curly tail, and a triangle for Cheesecake's bandanna on a piece of white construction paper or card stock. Color them in with colored pencils.

6. Cut out the paws, eyes, tail, and bandanna with scissors. Glue them onto Cheesecake, as shown.

7. Place Cheesecake on your construction paper or card stock. With a pencil, trace around Cheesecake to make a circle. Cut the circle out, and glue it to the bottom of Cheesecake so he can stand up!

Turn the page to make a bug buddy for your pom-pom mouse!

15

Blueberry Muffin's Blueberry Bug

This bug is Blueberry Muffin's favorite color—blue!

1. Collect the pom-poms that you'll need for your blueberry bug: one large blue pom-pom, one small white pom-pom, and one tiny light pink pom-pom.

What You Need

- 1 large (1 ½-inch) light blue pom-pom
- 1 small (¾-inch) white pom-pom
- 1 tiny light pink pom-pom
- Colored pencils
- 1 sheet of white construction paper
- Scissors
- White glue or craft glue
- Hole punch (optional)

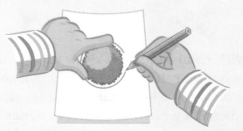

2. Use a colored pencil to draw a circle around the large blue pom-pom on a white sheet of construction paper. Cut out the circle and glue it to the bottom of the large pom-pom. This will help your bug stand up.

3. Glue the small white pom-pom on the blue one for your bug's head. Glue the tiny pink pom-pom on the white one for your bug's nose.

5. Use a hole punch to make some white dots from construction paper, or cut out some white dots with scissors. Glue them all over your bug's body for polka dots.

4. Draw two round eyes and a V-shaped antennae for your bug's head with colored pencils on the construction paper. Cut the shapes out and glue them to your bug's head.

Here's More: You can glue your Blueberry Bug on a clothespin or on a magnet for a berry cute decoration!

Turn the page to see how you can make your pom-poms bloom!

17

Pom-pom Picture Garden

Use pom-poms and yarn to make Blueberry Muffin's garden grow and bloom!

What You Need

- 1 sheet of light-colored construction paper
- Small pom-poms (3/4-inch, 8 yellow, 7 pink, 6 white)
- White glue or craft glue
- Pencil
- Pink yarn
- Scissors
- Crayons

1. Lay your light-colored sheet of construction paper sideways. Glue one pink and two yellow pom-poms to the paper, anywhere you like. These will be the centers of your flowers.

2. Glue six pom-poms around one center pom-pom. This makes one flower. Repeat with the other flower centers on your paper.

3. **With a pencil, draw two swirls on your paper. Outline the swirls with glue.**

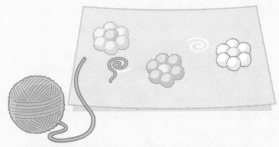

4. **Lay your pink yarn over the glue outline to make a pink swirl. Cut off any extra yarn. Repeat on the other swirl. Let dry.**

5. **Use a green crayon to draw leaves and stems on your yarn and pom-pom flowers.**

6. **Add a bright yellow sun to shine on your flower garden, and some fluffy white clouds.**

Here's More: You can make more flowers using your yarn! How about adding some tulips or daisies? It's up to you!

Turn the page to bake some of the best muffins in Strawberryland!

19

Berry Easy Blueberry Muffins

Blueberry Muffin bakes the best muffins in all of Strawberryland! You can bake yummy blueberry muffins just like she does with this easy recipe.

What You Need

- Muffin tin
- Cooking spray
- 2 cups flour
- ¾ cup sugar
- 2 teaspoons baking powder
- 1 teaspoon ground cinnamon
- ¼ teaspoon salt
- 2 eggs
- 1 cup milk
- ½ cup vegetable oil
- 1 cup blueberries (fresh or frozen)
- Utensils: Measuring cups and spoons, 2 large mixing bowls, spoons

Makes: 24 mini-muffins

1. Have an adult preheat the oven to 400°F. Coat your muffin tin with cooking spray.

2. In a mixing bowl, add the flour, sugar, baking powder, cinnamon, and salt. Stir with a spoon to get rid of any lumps.

3. In another mixing bowl, crack the eggs, then add the milk and vegetable oil. Stir until everything is mixed together.

4. Make a hole in the flour mixture with a spoon, and then pour the egg mixture into the hole. Stir just until the batter is mixed.

5. Fold the blueberries gently into the batter. Then, spoon the batter into the muffin tin, so that each cup is full.

6. Have an adult place the muffin tin in the oven. Bake your muffins for 20–30 minutes, or until they're golden brown. Let an adult remove the muffin tin from the oven and the muffins from the muffin tin. Let cool before eating.

Baking tip: If you're using frozen blueberries, just add the berries directly to the batter. You don't need to thaw them first!

Turn the page for more tasty muffins!

Blueberry Muffin's Tasty Muffin Variations

You can make lots of different kinds of muffins by replacing the blueberries in the muffin recipe with other fruit or fillings. Use your new fruit or filling in step 5 of the recipe on pages 20–21. Try some of these yummy ideas!

Banana Nut Muffins

Mash two ripe bananas and stir them into your batter. Fold in $\frac{1}{4}$ cup of chopped walnuts. Pour the batter into your muffin tin, and bake the muffins as directed.

Apple Cinnamon Muffins

Add 1 cup of chopped apple to your muffin batter. Pour the batter into your muffin tin, and bake as directed.

Lemon Poppy Seed Muffins

Squeeze the juice of two lemons into your batter (about $1/2$ cup of lemon juice). Add two tablespoons of poppy seeds, and stir. Pour the batter into your muffin tin, and bake as directed.

Chocolate Chip Muffins

Fold 1 cup of chocolate chips into your muffin batter. Pour the batter into the muffin tin, and bake as directed.

Peachy Fine Muffins

Drain a can of peach slices, and cut into bite-sized chunks. Fill the muffin cups $2/3$ full with batter. Top each muffin cup off with a peach chunk, and bake as directed.

Strawberry Surprise Muffins

Cut six strawberries in half and roll them in sugar to coat. Fill the muffin cups $2/3$ full with batter. Press a sugar-coated strawberry half into each cup, and bake as directed.

Turn the page for a berry starry sky—with butterflies!

Berry Stars and Butterflies

These stars and butterflies are made with our favorite fruits—strawberries and blueberries!

What You Need

- 5–6 strawberries
- ½ cup blueberries
- Utensils: Butter knife, cutting board, large plate

2. Take the leaves off the strawberries and slice them with your butter knife on a cutting board.

3. Place five strawberry slices on the plate to make a five-pointed star.

1. Wash your berries in cold water.

4. Fill the empty space in the middle of the star with blueberries. Repeat steps 3 and 4 to make another star.

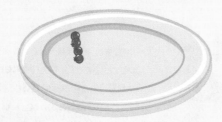

5. To make a butterfly, make a line using four blueberries for your butterfly's body.

Here's More: Use other fruits like grapes and apple slices to make more berry pretty creations! What other designs can you make?

6. Arrange four strawberry slices around the blueberry line for wings. Place blueberries on the wings for spots, if you like. Repeat steps 5 and 6 to make another butterfly.

Turn the page to shake up a berrylicious recipe!

Banana Blueberry Shake

Whip up this frosty drink for a quick sweet treat!

What You Need

- ½ cup frozen blueberries
- 1 banana, sliced
- ½ cup vanilla ice cream (about 2 scoops)
- ¼ cup milk
- 1 tablespoon honey
- Utensils: Measuring cups and spoons, ice cream scoop, blender, 2 glasses

Makes: 2 berrylicious servings

2. Let an adult blend the ingredients together, until they're smooth. If the shake is too thick, add a little milk and blend some more.

3. Pour the shake into two glasses, and enjoy!

Here's More: Try different berries or fruits in your shake, and mix it up!

1. Add the blueberries, banana, ice cream, milk, and honey to the blender.

What's red, blue, and all mixed up? Look on the next page to see!

Berry Mix-up

$\mathcal{M}$ix up your favorite berries for a berrylicious topping for ice cream or yogurt!

2. **Cover the bowl with plastic wrap and put it in the refrigerator to chill for 20 minutes.**

What You Need

- ½ cup strawberries, sliced
- ½ cup blueberries
- ½ cup raspberries
- 1 tablespoon sugar
- Vanilla ice cream or yogurt
- Utensils: Bowl, measuring spoon, spoon, plastic wrap

3. **Sprinkle your Berry Mix-up over ice cream or vanilla yogurt for a berry sweet treat!**

1. **Put the sliced strawberries, blueberries, and raspberries in a bowl. Sprinkle the sugar over the berries and toss.**

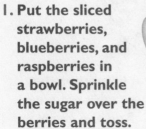

Turn the page for a cool and creamy dessert!

Blueberry Muffin's Berry Cool Cheesecake Cups

This easy, no-bake dessert is Cheesecake's favorite treat!

What You Need

- Graham crackers (5 sheets)
- Sealable plastic bag
- 2 (8-ounce) packages of cream cheese, softened
- 1 (14-ounce) can of sweetened condensed milk
- ½ lemon, juiced
- 1 teaspoon vanilla extract
- ½ cup strawberries, sliced
- ½ cup blueberries
- Utensils: Rolling pin (optional), mixing bowl, spoons, measuring cups and spoons, small bowls or cups, plastic wrap

Serves: 6 cool friends

1. Put the graham crackers in a sealable plastic bag. Use a rolling pin or your hands to break the crackers into small pieces.

2. To make the cheesecake filling, put the cream cheese into a bowl and beat with a spoon until it's smooth. Add the sweetened condensed milk little by little and stir, until everything is mixed together.

28

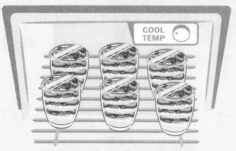

3. Stir the lemon juice and the vanilla into the cream cheese mixture.

6. Make five more cheesecake cups and cover each cup with plastic wrap. Chill your cheesecake cups for half an hour in the refrigerator. Enjoy with a spoon!

4. To make one cheesecake cup, put two tablespoons of the cream cheese mixture in a cup or small bowl, then sprinkle some graham cracker pieces on top.

5. Sprinkle a few slices of strawberries and a few of the blueberries over the graham crackers. Repeat steps 4 and 5 two more times to make two more layers.

Here's More: You can use other kinds of fruit in your Berry Cool Cheesecake Cups. What will you use? Peaches? Raspberries? It's up to you!

Turn the page to unscramble a muffin-baking mix-up!

A Berry Mixed-up Baking Day

Here are some mixed-up pictures from a blueberry-muffin baking day. Can you put these seven photos in the correct order by looking at each picture?

A.

Here we're pouring the batter into the muffin tin.

C.

Here we're letting the muffins cool.

B.

Mmmm! These muffins are berry yummy!

Answer on page 38.

D.

We washed our berries so they're sweet to eat.

F.

Here we're picking blueberries for our muffins.

E.

Here we're mixing the muffin batter.

G.

Here we're putting the muffins in the oven to bake.

Turn the page to make your berry own muffin basket!

31

Blueberry Muffin's Basket

Blueberry Muffin and I make these baskets to give out special treats—like yummy muffins from Blueberry's bakery, and sweet strawberries from my patch!

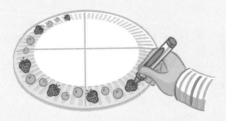

2. Decorate the back of the plate with crayons or markers. How will you decorate your basket? With blueberries or strawberries? Flowers? It's up to you!

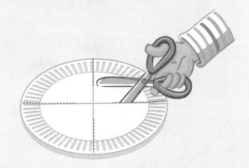

1. Fold a paper plate in half. Then fold the plate in half again. Open the paper plate to see your folds.

3. Turn the plate over so that the front side is up. Cut a slit halfway into the four folds you made in step 1, as shown.

32

4. Have an adult help you overlap two corners of two plate flaps so that they start to form a bowl shape. Staple in place.

7. Put a piece of waxed paper or a napkin in the bottom of your basket. Fill it with some freshly picked blueberries, yummy muffins, or other treats to give to a berry special friend!

5. Overlap and staple the rest of the paper flaps to form a bowl.

6. Use your pencil and a ruler to cut a 2-x-12-inch strip from a sheet of construction paper. Have an adult help you staple the ends to your basket to make a handle, as shown.

Turn the page for a cute muffin craft!

Blueberry Muffin's Photo Album

Take pictures of your friends and family to stitch together this special photo album that you can hang up!

What You Need

- Pencil
- Ruler
- Construction paper (blue and brown)
- Scissors
- Crayons
- White glue or craft glue
- Hole punch
- Pink yarn
- 4 photos of friends or family

1. Use your pencil and ruler to draw four 5-x-5-inch squares on sheets of blue construction paper. Cut them out.

2. Draw a muffin on a 4-x-4-inch square of brown construction paper. Cut it out. Trace around the muffin shape three more times on the brown paper for three more muffins. Cut them out.

3. Decorate your muffins with crayons. Add spots for blueberries or chocolate chips. What kind of muffins will you make? It's up to you!

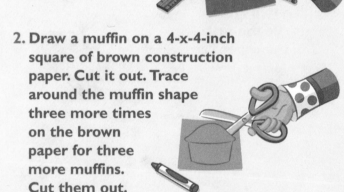

4. **Glue one muffin to each square of blue paper. Let dry.**

5. **Lay your squares out in the order that you'd like. In the first square, use the hole punch to punch three holes in the bottom of the square. On the last square, punch three holes in the top edge. Punch holes in the top and bottom of the two middle squares.**

6. **Thread yarn through two holes in two squares, as shown. Tie a knot in the back.**

7. **Thread the yarn through the rest of the holes, sewing the two squares together. Once you come to the end, tie a knot and cut the yarn. Sew the rest of the squares together, just like you did in steps 6 and 7, so that all of them are connected.**

8. **Trim your photos so that each picture will fit inside one muffin. Glue each picture to the muffin.**

Here's More: Hang up your photo album on a door or wall in your room.

Turn the page to make a place to hang your pretty art projects!

35

Blueberry Muffin and I use this project to display our cute crafts!

1. Draw a leaf shape on a sheet of green construction paper about 2 inches long with a green crayon. Cut the leaf out. Draw and cut out seven more leaves.

2. Draw a blueberry on a blue sheet of construction paper with a blue crayon. Cut it out. Draw and cut out three more blueberries.

What You Need

- Construction paper (blue and green)
- Crayons (blue and green)
- Scissors
- 4 wooden clothespins
- White glue or craft glue
- Cord or shoelace (about 4 feet long)
- 2 pushpins

3. Glue two leaves onto a wooden clothespin. Let dry.

4. Glue a blueberry on top of the leaves on the clothespin. Let dry. Repeat steps 3 and 4 with the rest of the clothespins.

Here's More: You can use your artwork line to hang up your favorite photos, or use it to display greeting cards. What else can you hang on your artwork line?

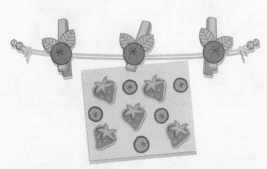

5. Have a grown-up help you hang a cord on the wall with two pushpins. Clip the clothespins on the cord. Use the clothespins to hang up your favorite art projects!

Blueberry Muffin's Answer Page

Blueberry Muffin's Blue Words (pages 12–13)

1. blueberries
2. sky
3. ocean or river
4. blue whale
5. blue jeans
6. blue jay

A Berry Mixed-up Baking Day (pages 30–31)

Step 1

F.

Step 2

D.

Step 3

E.

Step 4

A.

Step 5

G.

Step 6

C.

Step 7

B.

More Sweet Strawberryland Adventures COMING SOON!

To Our Berry Sweet Friend,

We're so glad that you came with us on this berry blue adventure! Blueberry Muffin and I had lots of fun sharing muffin recipes, crafts, and games with you. See you again soon!

Your berry best friends,

Strawberry Shortcake,

BLUEBERRY MUFFIN,

and CHEESECAKE 🐰

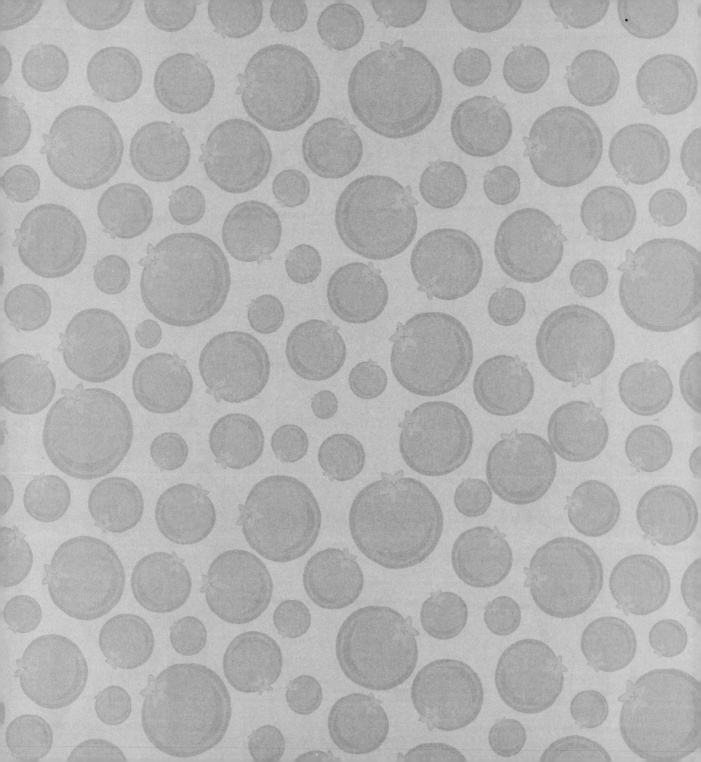